Hank snaps.

My hair began to rise and my ears jumped to the Full Alert position. My eyes narrowed to slits and my lips began to twitch and my teeth exposed themselves in all their frightening glory.

I heard a loud R-I-P! This was intolerable, unbearable.

All at once I was finding it very hard to . . . the cat was not only defacing Sally May's sheet, but in a deeper sense he was committing a senseless act of senseless vandalism against MY RANCH!

Okay, that was it.

Red Alert, full throttle, all systems go, open fire, launch all torpedoes, charge, bonzai! THIS WAS WAR!!

The Case of the Missing Cat

The Case of the Missing Cat

John R. Erickson

Illustrations by Gerald L. Holmes

Puffin Books

PUFFIN BOOKS
Published by the Penguin Group
Penguin Putnam Books for Young Readers,
345 Hudson Street, New York, New York 10014, U.S.A.
Penguin Books Ltd,
27 Wrights Lane, London W8 5TZ, England
Penguin Books Australia Ltd,
Ringwood, Victoria, Australia
Penguin Books Canada Ltd,
10 Alcorn Avenue, Toronto, Ontario, Canada M4V 3B2
Penguin Books (N.Z.) Ltd,
182-190 Wairau Road, Auckland 10, New Zealand

Penguin Books Ltd, Registered Offices:
Harmondsworth, Middlesex, England

First published in the United States of America
by Maverick Books, Gulf Publishing Company, 1990
Published by Puffin Books, a member of
Penguin Putnam Books for Young Readers, 1999

13 15 17 19 20 18 16 14

LIBRARY OF CONGRESS CATALOGING-IN-PUBLICATION DATA
Erickson, John R., date
The case of the missing cat / John R. Erickson ;
illustrations by Gerald L. Holmes.
p. cm.
Previously published: Houston, Tex. : Maverick Books, c1990.
(Hank the Cowdog ; 15)
Summary: Pete the barncat swindles the intrepid cowdog
out of his job as Head of Ranch Security.
978-0-14-130391-8
[1. Dogs Fiction. 2. Cats Fiction. 3. Ranch life—West (U.S.) Fiction.
4. West (U.S.) Fiction. 5. Humorous stories.]
I. Holmes, Gerald L., ill. II. Title. III. Series: Erickson, John R., date
Hank the Cowdog ; 15
[PZ7.E72556Camk 1999] [Fic]—dc21 99-19574 CIP

Hank the Cowdog® is a registered trademark of John R. Erickson.

Printed in the United States of America

Dedicated to the memory of my father,
Joseph W. Erickson

CONTENTS

Chapter One Pete's Con Game **1**

Chapter Two Pete Makes a Foolish Wager **11**

Chapter Three The Case of the Lumber-Pile Bunny **20**

Chapter Four The Bunny Cheats and Lies **29**

Chapter Five Humble Pie Stinks **38**

Chapter Six The Case of the Disheartened Chicken **48**

Chapter Seven Bloody Writing on the Wall **58**

Chapter Eight The Healing Waters of Emerald Pond **68**

Chapter Nine Pete's Mindless Senseless Vandalism of a Sheet **76**

Chapter Ten The Infamous Black Hole of Mustard **86**

Chapter Eleven Total Happiness Without Pete **96**

Chapter Twelve Happy Endings Aren't as Simple as You Might Think **104**

CHAPTER ONE

Pete's Con Game

It's me again, Hank the Cowdog. Have I ever mentioned that I don't like cats? I don't like cats.

And the cat I don't like the most, the cat I dislike with my whole entire body and soul, is a certain selfish, sneaking, lazy, never-sweat character on my ranch named Pete the Barncat.

You see, it was Pete who lured me into the Case of the Lumber-Pile Bunny. That was the straw that broke the camel's tooth and set my wicked mind to plotting ways of...

Hmmm. How can I say this so that it doesn't sound crude and tacky? I decided, don't you see, that our ranch would be a happier and more wholesome place if Pete were suddenly to... well, vanish, you might say. Without a trace.

1

No clues. No suspects. No way that Sally May could connect me with the, uh, tragedy.

But I'm getting ahead of myself. Better start at the beginning.

It was mid-morning, fall of the year, as I recall. I was making my way around the yard fence, heading toward the front of the house, when I encountered Pete the Barncat and my assistant, Mister Half-Stepper, Mister Sleep-Till-Noon, Mister Look-at-the-Clouds. Drover.

They were sitting across from one another, looking down at the ground between them. Their behavior struck me as suspicious. I mean, at a distance of ten or twelve feet I could see nothing on the ground between them—nothing but dirt, that is—so why were they looking at dirt?

I put my primary mission on temporary hold, altered course, and went over to check this thing out.

"Number One, what's going on around here? Number Two, you're supposed to be resting up for night patrol, Drover. Number Three, mingling with cats is against regulations."

Drover's head came up and he gave me his patented silly grin. "Oh, hi Hank, we're playing checkers."

"Playing checkers?" I moved closer. "It's odd

that you should say that, Drover, because I don't see either a checkerboard or checkers."

"That's because we're playing Checkerless Checkers, aren't we, Pete?"

The cat grinned and nodded. "That's right, Hankie. We're playing Checkerless Checkers. Want to play?"

"Negative. Not only do I not want to play Checkerless Checkers, I don't believe there's any such game. And if there's no such game, I refuse to play it, period."

Pete shrugged and turned his attention to the ground. He moved his paw across the phony so-called "checkerboard," tapping it in three different places.

"Sorry, Drover, but I just jumped three of your men."

Drover squinted at the ground. "Oh darn. I guess I shouldn't have made that move. Did I lose another game?"

Pete nodded and grinned. "Um-hmmm, you did, but you're getting better all the time. You sure you don't want to play the winner, Hankie?"

I pushed Drover aside and moved in closer. "Okay, I've seen enough to know that there's something fishy going on here. Drover, where did you learn this so-called game?"

"Well, let's see. Right here on the ranch."

"From who or whom did you learn it?"

"Well, let's see. From Pete."

"In other words, your only knowledge of the rules of this so-called game came from Pete, is that correct?"

"Well, let's see." He squinted one eye and rolled the other one around. "I guess that's right."

I began pacing. "Very good. Next question. Are

you telling me that you can remember every move in a checker game?"

"Well, I can't but Pete can."

"How do you know that?"

"He told me so."

"I see." I glanced from one face to the other. The pieces of the puzzle began falling into place. "One more question, Drover, and I'll have this thing wrapped up. Which of you has won more games?"

Drover looked at the sky. "Let's see. Pete won the first one. And Pete won the second one. But Pete won the fourth one. And then Pete won the fifth one."

"Hold it right there. You failed to mention who won the crucial third game."

"I think Pete won that one."

"Hm, yes."

I paced around the two of them. Drover watched me until his head went as far to the south as it could go without coming unscrewed, and at that point he fell over backward.

"Get up, Drover, and listen carefully. I've found a pattern here."

He struggled back to a sitting position. "Oh good."

"Does it strike you as odd that Pete has won

five out of five games? Did it ever occur to you that Pete might be cheating?"

"Oh heck no. We promised that we wouldn't cheat."

Pete was still grinning and had begun to purr. "That's right, Hankie. We both promised not to cheat, because cheating isn't nice."

Suddenly I stopped pacing and whirled around. "It's all clear now, Drover, and I can tell you what's been going on. You've been duped. This cat lured you into a game you couldn't possibly win, and he has cheated you."

"But he promised . . ."

"Never mind what he promised. Cats always cheat. You can write that down in your little book."

"I don't have a little book."

"Get one. I'm ashamed of you, Drover. Only a chump would play Checkerless Checkers with a cat."

"Well . . . we had fun."

"Exactly, and having fun is one of the many things we're not allowed to do in the Security Business. Speaking of which, since you've spent most of the morning goofing off, why don't you go down to the corrals and check things out."

"We can't play another game?"

"That's correct, because I'm closing it down. This cat is through, finished."

"Oh drat. I was just catching on."

"Go! And I'll expect a full report in twenty minutes."

Little Drover went padding down toward the gas tanks. When he was gone, I turned to Pete. He was doodling around on the so-called checkerboard with his left front paw. His tail stuck straight up in the air and the end of it was twitching back and forth.

"Pete, you ought to be ashamed of yourself, taking advantage of a dunce."

"It's hard to fool you, Hankie."

"Not just hard, Pete. Impossible. I had your con game figgered out the minute I walked up here. Playing checkers without checkers! I can't believe you talked the poor little mutt into that."

"You never know until you try."

I studied the cat for a long time. "Pete, there's a certain understanding between creeps like you and a dog like me. It's like cops and robbers. Only the cops know how good the robbers are in their shabby work, and only the robbers know how good the cops are."

"That's right, Hankie. You understand me and I understand you."

"Exactly. We're on opposite sides of the law, we're sworn enemies, and yet we can't help admiring each other's work."

"Um-hm. I learned long ago that I couldn't put anything over on the Head of Ranch Security."

"Exactly. We'll never be friends, Pete. Fate has taken care of that. But in a crazy sort of way . . . what are you doing?"

He had swept his paw over the so-called checkerboard, and now he appeared to be . . . I wasn't sure what he was doing.

"Oh I'm through with the checker game. I know it won't work on you."

"That's correct, but what are you doing?"

After clearing the board of so-called checkers, he appeared to be . . . setting it up again?

He looked at me with his lazy cattish eyes. "I thought I might play a game of chess—with myself."

"Chess?"

"That's right. You've probably never heard of it. It's a very complicated game that requires concentration and . . ."

I couldn't help smiling. "Pete, is it possible that you think I don't know about chess? The ancient game of war, invented thousands of years ago by the Balonians? Which requires cunning and intel-

8

ligence? Hey, I've got bad news for you, cat. I know ALL about chess. Ask me anything."

"Black or white?"

"Huh?"

"Would you rather play black or white?"

"Oh. Black, I suppose. It matches the color of my heart."

"All right. I'll open with pawn to king four."

"Oh yeah?" I hunkered down and studied the board. "Well, that doesn't scare me at all, cat, and I'll move this little fawn out here."

"It's a *pawn,* Hankie, not a fawn."

"Whatever. There's my move. Weed it and reap."

Five minutes later, I was in deep trouble, I had lost three bishops, one knight, and my castle was in check. And at that very moment, I realized Drover was standing beside me.

He stared at us. "What are you doing?"

I looked at Drover. I looked at Pete. I looked down at the empty space of dirt between us. It occurred to me that . . . I swept my paw across the so-called chessboard, erasing all traces of the so-called game.

"We were studying the dirt, Drover, talking soil samples, you might say, and what are you doing back so soon?"

"I just wanted to tell you that I saw a cotton-

9

tail rabbit. He was eating grass right in front of our gunnysack beds."

"You're bothering me with a report about a rabbit? I'm a busy dog, Drover, and I have no time for . . ."

It was then that I realized that Pete had disappeared. I glanced around and saw him—creeping down the hill TOWARD MY COTTONTAIL RABBIT!

CHAPTER TWO

Pete Makes a Foolish Wager

It didn't take me long to catch up with Pete. "Hold it right there, cat. It appears to me that you're moving toward a certain cottontail rabbit. Before you get yourself into some serious trouble, I should point out that the alleged rabbit belongs to me."

"Oh really? I thought you were too busy for rabbits, Hankie."

"I was misquoted. What I meant to say was that the rabbit belongs to me and you can keep your paws off of him."

"Now Hankie, be reasonable. You don't have any use for a rabbit."

"Oh yeah? Says who?"

"In the first place, he's not bothering anyone.

He's just a cute, innocent little bunny who's eating grass."

"Yeah, but it's MY grass, see, and he's down there by MY gunnysack and he doesn't have a permit to eat my grass in the vicinity of my gunnysack."

Pete grinned and licked his front paw with a long stroke of his tongue. "And in the second place, it's a well-known fact that a dog can't catch a rabbit."

I stared at the cat and began laughing. *"A dog can't catch a rabbit?* Is that what you just said?"

"Um-hmm, because a dog goes about it the wrong way. Instead of being patient and stalking the rabbit, as a cat would do, a dog just blunders in and starts chasing."

"Blunders in and starts chasing, huh? Go on, cat, I'm dying to hear the rest of this."

"Mmmm, all right. And once the rabbit starts running, the game is over because a dog can't catch a rabbit on the run. That's a well-known fact."

"No, Pete, that's well-known garbage, just the sort of half-truth and gossip that a cat would spread around. What you're saying is so outrageous that I refuse to discuss it any more."

"Whatever you think, Hankie."

"Except to repeat what I've already said: Leave my rabbit alone. Now, if you'll excuse me, I've got . . ."

"I'll bet you can't catch him."

". . . two weeks' work lined up for . . . what did you just say?"

"I'll bet you can't catch him."

I lowered my nose until it was only inches away from the cat's face. "You want to bet me that I can't catch a sniveling little cottontail rabbit? On

13

my ranch? When I'm Head of Ranch Security?"

"Um-hmmm."

My first thought was to meet his challenge head-on, take him up on his foolish bet, and settle the matter once and for all time. However...

It was too easy. Something was wrong here.

See, when you've worked around cats as much as I have, you develop a certain degree of caution. They're stupid animals, but they're stupid in a cunning sort of way.

They have a talent for twisting things around. It's a minor talent, it doesn't compare at all with the larger and grander talents you'll find in even your average breed of dogs, and I'm talking about, oh, just to mention a few: good looks, high intelligence, courage, tremendous physical strength, good looks, speed, quickness, determination, endurance, and devilish good looks.

I must give Beulah the Collie most of the credit for spotting those qualities in ... well, ME, you might say. Otherwise I might never have known they were there, which would have been a real shame.

Where was I?

Funny how Beulah seems to creep into my thoughts, but I was talking about something else, seems to me, and ...

Oh yes, cats. They have this minor talent for twisting things around, and over the years I've learned that when a cat makes a simple statement or says something that appears on the surface to make sense, it's time to pull back and study the deal from a different prospectus.

I walked a short distance away and switched over into Heavy Duty Analysis Mode.

Pete had just offered to make a foolish wager with me, one which he had no chance of winning. Now, why would a cat do such a thing?

Answer #1: The cat is just dumb, and you must expect a dumb cat to make dumb mistakes.

Answer #2: The cat is dumb, but not quite as dumb as he appears to be, in which case he should be approached with caution.

Answer #3: The cat is actually pretty smart and . . . I didn't need to follow this one out any further because it was too outrageous to consider. I mean, this was the same cat who had invented a nonexistent game called "Checkerless Checkers," right? Nothing more needed to be said.

And so, having dismissed Answer #3 in record time, I ran Answer #1 and Answer #2 through my data banks. What the printout revealed was a confirmation of Answer #1, which I had suspected all along.

Pete had made a dumb mistake and had thrown down the goblet, so to speak, and challenged me to enter into a foolish wager. Foolish for Pete, that is.

Okay, the only question left to ask was, "Would Hank the Cowdog consider taking unfair advantage of a dumb cat?" And I didn't need to run that one through the data banks.

In a word YES. I would, with all my heart and soul.

Stealing glances as I paced back and forth, I studied the cat, measured him, sized him up, and prepared my next move. A strategy began to take shape in my mind, and at that point I was ready to respond.

I swaggered back over to him. "Okay, I'll take you up on your bet, kitty, but only if there's something at stake."

He looked up at me with his big cattish eyes. "Hmmm. You mean something valuable?"

"Exactly. I don't enter into bets with cats for my health. If you can't put up something that makes this deal worth my time and trouble, I'm not interested."

"My goodness, Hankie, you get pretty serious about these things, don't you?"

"You got that right, cat. I'm a very busy dog

16

and the nickel-and-dime stuff doesn't interest me."

"Well, let me think. I'll bet you tonight's supper scraps."

"Not enough."

"Well, then I'll throw in tomorrow's breakfast scraps too."

"To be real blunt about it, Pete, scraps don't excite me right now. If we're going to bet, I want to bet something that really matters—something that, if lost, will hurt BAD."

"Ummm! That kind of bet!"

I smirked and gave him a worldly, sideways glance. "Now you understand, Pete. No penny ante here. This is go-for-broke. Do you want into the deal or do you want out?"

He studied his claws for a moment, I mean, the cat was obviously scared and stalling for time. "All right, Hankie, if that's the way you want it."

"That's the way I want it."

His eyes came up. "I'll bet you your job as Head of Ranch Security."

"HUH? My job as . . . now wait just a minute."

"You wanted big stakes, right? You wanted to go for broke, right?"

"Yeah, but . . ."

"There's the bet," he grinned, "if you're dog enough to take it."

My eyes narrowed and a growl began to rumble deep in my throat. "Watch what you say, cat. Your words could come back to honk you. And if your words don't honk you loud enough, I might consider doing a little honking of my own. Repeat the bet."

"I'm betting your job as Head of Ranch Security that you can't catch that rabbit."

My data banks whirred. "Let me get this straight. If I lose, you get my job as Head of Ranch Security. But what are you putting up? What happens if you lose?"

"Well, if I lose, you win the job as Head of Ranch Security. We'll both be playing for the same prize, and if the prize is the same for both of us, it has to be a fair bet."

I didn't like the way he was grinning, so I took the time to study the deal from every possible angle. It checked out. For the first time in years, this cat had offered a deal that was equal, fair, square, level, and plumb.

"All right, cat, you've got yourself a bet. It's a done deal and there will be no backing out."

"You only get three tries."

"Sure, fine, don't bore me with details."

"But what if you lose, Hankie? Will you pay off?"

I laughed. "That's not likely to happen, Kitty, but if it does, I'll pay off. You've got my Solemn Cowdog Oath on it."

"Mmmm. And a cowdog never goes against his oath, right?"

"Exactly. And now that you've committed yourself to the deal, I can reveal that you've made a very foolish blunder. Pete, old buddy, old pal, you're fixing to lose it all on one roll of the dice."

He gasped! Yes, he tried to hide it but I saw him gasp. Hey, that cat was beginning to feel the jaws of my trap closing around him.

All that remained was for me to lumber down and catch the rabbit, which would be a piece of cake for this old dog. I mean, catching rabbits was no big deal for me—just by George run 'em down and snatch 'em up in the old iron jaws.

Yes sir, and when that happened, fellers, Pete the Barncat would be out of luck and out of business.

CHAPTER THREE

The Case of the Lumber-Pile Bunny

As you might expect, old Pete was shaking in his tracks, and we're talking about worried sick and scared to death.

I guess he'd finally figgered out that he'd bet his entire future on this deal and that his chances of winning had come down to Slim and None.

Slim Chances, not Slim the Cowboy. There are several Slims around here, don't you see.

Anyways, I headed down to the gas tanks to find the Lumber-Pile Bunny.

Did I mention where he got his name? Maybe not. Okay, here we go.

One of my jobs on the ranch was to identify and track the movements of every rabbit within the perimeter of ranch headquarters. At that particular time, I was following the movements of three alleged rabbits: the one we called the Cake-House Bunny, who stayed under the cake house; the Cattle-Guard Bunny, who lived in the cattle guard just north of headquarters; and the Lumber-Pile Bunny.

I knew them all on sight, had memorized their markings and habits, and had been keeping all of them under pretty close surveillance for months and months.

"How could one dog keep track of three rabbits at the same time?" you ask. Good question. All I can say is that I did it. A lot of dogs would have found it difficult, if not impossible, but for me, it was just part of the job.

The next thing you're probably asking yourself is, "Where did the Lumber-Pile Bunny get his name?" Another good question.

I had assigned the code name "Lumber-Pile Bunny" to this particular rabbit because . . . well, because he lived in a lumber pile, and maybe that was fairly obvious. But there was nothing obvious about where the lumber pile came from.

Here's the scoop on that. Back in the spring, the cowboys became so embarrassed by the appearance of their corral fence that they took the drastic step of replacing twenty or thirty rotten, warped, moth-eaten boards with new lumber.

Any time those guys give up on using a baling wire patch the action can be regarded as drastic. Yes, they did in fact replace the old boards with new boards, but did they *haul off the old boards?*

No sir. Throwed 'em in a pile on the west side and drove away, saying, "We'll haul that lumber off when we get caught up with some of this other work." But did they? No sir.

That's a pretty sorry way to run a ranch, seems to me, but did anyone ask the opinion of the Head of Ranch Security? Again, NO. I'll say no more about it.

Except that lumber piles attract rattlesnakes and skunks and provide a place of refuse for sniveling little rabbits, speaking of whom . . .

Would you care to guess who took up residence in the lumber pile? That's correct, a certain cottontail rabbit, to who or whom I assigned the code name "Lumber-Pile Bunny." This was the guy I was after.

Okay. Some ten feet north of the gas tanks, I throttled back to a slow gliding walk, switched my ears over to Manual Liftup, began testing the air with full nosetory equipment, and directed my VSD's (Visual Scanning Devices; in ordinary dogs also referred to as "eyes") toward a patch of grass directly west of the gas tanks.

This procedure soon bored fruit . . . bared fruit . . . produced results, as my instruments began picking up the telltale sounds of a rabbit munching grass.

It was the Lumber-Pile Bunny.

He was munching tender shoots of grass some 25 or 30 feet to the west of my bedroom. The foolish rabbit seemed unaware that he had entered a Secured Area and that the Dark Shadow of Doom was slipping toward him like a dark shadow in the night.

Well, maybe not in the night. You wouldn't be able to see a dark shadow in the . . .

Even though I had switched over to Silent Mode, the bunny heard me coming. They have pretty good ears, don't you know, and it's hard to slip up on one.

But get this. Instead of running away, he stood up on his back legs, looked straight at me, and wiggled his nose in what I would describe as "a provocatory gesture."

Okay, what we had here was a rabbit who had never been taught his place on the ranch. Or else one that had lost his mind. He wanted to play with fire, so he was fixing to learn about fire.

Well, this was it. I glanced back to be sure that Pete was watching (he was), took a deep breath, and rolled my shoulders several times to loosen up the enormous muscles that would soon propel me at speeds unknown to ordinary dogs.

I turned back to the rabbit, locked in all guidance systems, and began the countdown procedure, which goes something like this, in case you're not familiar with technical stuff:

"Five! Four! Three! Two! One! Launch, liftoff, charge, bonzai!!"

And in a puff of smoke and a cloud of dust, I went streaking toward the target.

Rabbits are famous for their speed, right? What many people don't know is that your better grades of cowdog are every bit as fast as a rabbit, and in a few rare cases (me, for example) are even faster.

I'm not one to boast, but speed was just built into my bloodline.

In other words, the Lumber-Pile Bunny was in big trouble from the very beginning. I closed in on him fast and was only inches away from snapping him up in my jaws when . . .

Let's call it luck. He got lucky, that's all. And why not? After all, he was carrying around four lucky rabbit's feet.

Luck kept him a couple of feet ahead of me as we went streaking out into the home pasture. Inches, actually. We made a wide loop, some 25 yards in front of the corrals, and then I realized that Bunny had changed directions and was high-balling it straight to the lumber pile.

It was an old rabbit trick. I recognized it right away and took appropriate measures. I went to Incredible Speed and . . . like I said, he was carrying four lucky rabbit's feet.

I never denied that rabbits are pretty swift and, okay, maybe he beat me to the lumber pile, but not by much. If the chase had gone another ten feet, I would have nailed him.

I returned to the gas tanks to wait for him to come out again, as I knew he would. Off to the north, I heard a familiar whiny voice say, "Mmmm, that's one, Hankie."

"Don't worry about it, Kitty, that was just a warm-up."

I waited. And waited. The minutes dragged by. Perhaps I dozed. Then . . . the munching of grass reached my ears. He was back, same place. Munching grass right in front of my bedroom. Foolish rabbit.

Within seconds I had gone through the launch procedure and was back on the chase. You should

have seen me! Made that loop out into the pasture and virtually destroyed three acres of good buffalo grass and virtually had that bunny trapped in the deadly vice of my jaws, and if the chase had gone another five feet, that little feller would have been a stasstistic.

Stasstisstic.

History.

Real close race, almost got him, a huge improvement over the first run, and as long as a guy can see improvement, he knows that he has won a moral victory. And so, with a victory hanging in the trophy room of my mind, I returned, triumphant and victorious, to the gas tanks.

A little winded, yes, but beneath the huffing and puffing was the warm glow of satisfaction that comes when a dog knows he's done his job right.

"Mmmm, that's two, Hankie," said the cat. "Only one shot left."

I chuckled and didn't bother to reply. I knew what the cat was trying to do—put pressure on me so that I would choke. What he didn't know was that some dogs *thrive* on pressure, I mean, it's like throwing gasoline into a . . .

CHOKE! GASP! ARG!

On the other hand, I was beginning to feel a small amount of . . . I mean, my job, my position, my entire career was riding on the next . . .

WHEEZE! ARG! GASP!

Holy smokes, if I didn't catch the rabbit on the next run, *Pete the Barncat would be the next Head of Ranch Security!* Not only would that be a personal disaster for me personally, but it would be disaster for the entire ranch.

Gulp.

Pressure. It weighs heavy on the mind, smashes creative impulses, crushes the little flowers of courage that try to bloom in the warm soil of . . . something.

I was curled up in a ball, in the process of pretending that I was a puppy again, back in the sweet days before I had assumed all the crushing responsibilities of running a ranch, when all of a sudden . . .

I lifted my eyes and narrowed my head . . . lifted my head and narrowed my eyes, I should say, and there sat the Lumber-Pile Bunny, not ten feet in front of me.

Okay, this was it. My whole career had come down to this moment, this last chase.

I arose from my gunnysack bed and prepared myself for what was sure to be the most important mission of my life.

CHAPTER FOUR

The Bunny Cheats and Lies

"**G**ood luck, Hankie. Is there anything I should be doing to prepare for my new position?"

That was Pete the Barncat, trying to use underhanded sneaky tricks to shake my confidence. I tried to ignore him, which is the second-best thing you can do with a cat.

The first-best thing you can do with a cat is to beat the snot out of him and run him up a tree, which I sincerely wanted to do but couldn't, for the simple reason that I had an appointment with Destiny.

This was my last chance, fellers, and I had to put everything into it. Hence, instead of rushing off and wasting my last shot, I decided to analyze the two previous attempts and try to learn from my . . .

I wouldn't exactly call them *mistakes*. Errors might be a better word.

Bad luck.

Difficulties.

Unfortunate circumstances.

Tiny miscalculations.

Windows of opportunity that had been slammed shut by the winds of Life.

Circumstances beyond the control of myself or any other dog on earth.

I decided to learn from the past, shall we say.

For you see, I had detected a certain pattern in the bunny's response to my missions against him. Here, look at this map. Oh well, you can't see it.

Okay, imagine a map. The gas tanks form Point A, right here. The lumber pile becomes Point B, over here. Point C is the point in the home pasture to which the bunny had run on the two previous encounters.

As you can see, the three points, if joined together by imaginary lines A Prime, B Prime, and Prime Rib, would form a triangle.

Pretty suspicious, huh? How did that rabbit know about triangles? How could he have known that if you connect any three points in the universe with straight lines, you get a triangle?

I mean, we're talking about geometry—the

kind of heavy duty math we use all the time in the Security Business, but not the sort of thing you'd expect a bunny rabbit to understand.

This was my first hint that perhaps I had underestimated the intelligence of the alleged rabbit. Not only had he won the first two outings against me, but there appeared to be more than a slim chance *that his victories could be traced to something other than dumb luck.*

In other words, I was staring right into the jaws of a conspiracy. This rabbit had been using strategy against me, and to explain what I mean, let's go back to the map.

I'm here at Point A. The rabbit is right in front of me. He takes off toward Point B. I follow him, pursuing a course described by line A Prime.

You still with me? I know this is pretty complicated stuff but just hang on.

Okay, Bunny reaches Point B in the pasture. What does he do then? He changes directions and goes streaking toward Point C, the lumber pile, following line B Prime.

Here's the startling conclusion of all this. It was beginning to appear that the rabbit had led me to Point B, KNOWING ALL THE TIME THAT HE WOULD END UP RUNNING BACK TO THE LUMBER PILE!

Now, if that's not cheating, tell me what is. It's the kind of backhanded, underhanded, lefthanded, sneaking approach you'd expect from a cat—but from an innocent little rabbit? No sir.

Hey, if you can't trust a rabbit anymore, what kind of world are we living in? What are we coming to?

I mean, once the rabbits turn to lying and cheating, who's next? The kids? Mothers? Baby birds? Puppy dogs and fawns? Apple pie? Christmas carols?

Is there anything sacred left in a world where bunny rabbits lie and cheat and steal and rob and spit at their grandmothers?

Just when I think I've seen it all, I see something else. Just when I think I've hardened myself as hard as I can harden, I find fresh evidence of something new and awful. Just when I think this soiled world has no more shocks and surprises, I see something like this, and it just about breaks my heart.

Rabbits cheating. Rabbits lying.

Well . . . a guy can't just quit or resign from Life or crawl under his gunnysack and hide from all the meanness and ugliness. He's got to come back and strike a few blows for Honesty and Decency.

And that's where I found myself, after going through several minutes of spiritual heartburn and moral agony. I couldn't change the world, fellers, or put all the bad guys out of business or spare the little children from the mess we'd made of the world.

All I could do was catch that stupid, stinking, sniveling, sneaking, counterfeit little rabbit who had made a fool out of me, not once but twice, and teach him an important lesson about lying and cheating.

What a fool I'd been! I'd played the role of Mister Nice Dog and what had it gotten me? Okay, he wanted to play games with me, so we'd play games. But we were fixing to play MY game.

Here's the crutch of the whole matter. I'll reveal it if you promise not to blab it around. See, that rabbit was more devious than I'd ever supposed. He'd made that loop out into the pasture, knowing all along that I would follow him.

Heh heh, but just suppose that I didn't follow him. Just suppose that instead of running my legs off out in the pasture, I took a shortcut through the corrals and was standing in front of the lumber pile when he came hopping up. Heh heh.

Pretty awesome, huh? Let me tell you something. I hadn't been named Head of Ranch Security strictly on my good looks, although that had been a big factor.

A dog's mind is a scary thing, and moral indigestion is a powerful force. Put 'em together and you have something that is truly awesome.

Okay, here we go. I rose from my gunnysack bed, just as I had done before, and began the Pursuit Phase of the procedure. The bunny ran. I chased. We headed out into the pasture and began the Sucker Phase.

I was watching the rabbit very carefully this time, don't you see, and when he stopped looking back over his shoulder, I altered my compass heading, veered off hard to the right, and went zooming straight for the corral fence.

As I approached the fence, I did one last instrument check. Allowing for wind and so forth, I would arrive at the lumber pile three seconds before the victim.

All systems were go. All I had to do now was perform what we call an Under-the-Bottom-Board-Maneuver, a fairly simple and routine procedure in which your cowdog approaches a corral fence at top speed and darts under your bottom 2 x 6 board without

CRUNCH!!

Uh.

Uhhh.

Uhhhhhhh!

Lorkin @#$%&*?%$#@ murgle porkchop snicklefritz aimed a wee bit high on that one. Swimming in molasses, the stars came out gork murg snork and I gathered myself up off of the...

I became aware of a throbbing pain in my head. My neck was badly cricked and someone had removed my legs and installed a new set made of soft rubber. The earth was turning in an odd direction and I found it hard to stand in one spot.

It appeared that I had, or shall we say that my instruments had failed me at a very crucial point in the maneuver, and once your entire guidance system has gone on the fritz . . .

Laughter? Did I hear . . . yes, the cowboys. Laughing. Howling. Leaning against the saddle shed. Doubled over. Slapping their thighs.

They had been spying on me, had watched the entire incident. Did they rush out with ice packs or bandages or even an encouraging word? Oh no. Everything's a big joke with them.

"Go get that little rabbit, Hankie!" one of them yelled. I don't remember which one, it doesn't matter, I don't care, one's as bad as the other and neither one shows much sensitivity to tragic situations.

"Sic 'im, boy!" said the other, as he was brought to his knees by a convulsion of childish laughter.

So there I was—not only badly injured from wounds received on a combat mission, not only wrecked and deformed and partly crippled, but also mocked and scorned by the very people I had sworn my Cowdog Oath to protect.

Maybe you think I had hit the absolute bottom, that I couldn't stink any deeper, sink any deeper, I should say; maybe you think that every-thing bad that could have happened to me had happened to me.

If that's what you think, then you've forgotten that I had wagered my job as Head of Ranch Security and HAD LOST THE WAGER.

In other words, fellers, not only had I lost my job but it had been won by Pete the Barncat.

That's what I'd call a pretty scary thought.

CHAPTER FIVE

Humble Pie Stinks

W ell, the cowboys got a real lift out of my disaster. I mean, it just about made their whole day.

After howling and chuckling and slapping their knees and rolling around in the dirt, they finally ran out of excuses for loafing and had to go back to work. I know that broke their hearts.

And don't forget that if they had hauled off that pile of junk lumber in the first place, there would have been no lumber pile and therefore no Lumber-Pile Bunny.

Hence, by simple logic, we see that the cowboys were actually to blame for the entire incident—which didn't make my broken neck or damaged head feel one bit better, but it's always nice to share the blame with someone else.

I mean, sharing is a very important thing in this old life. Furthermore, there is a wise old saying about people who laugh at the misfortunes of others: "He who laughs first . . . he who laughs last . . . he who laughs in the middle . . ."

There is this wonderful wise old saying about people laughing but I think we'll skip it for now. It's a real good wise old . . . never mind.

I went limping back to the gas tanks. I mean, I'd just suffered one of the worst setbacks of my career and had lost just about everything that was dear to me, but I still had my old gunnysack bed.

That was the one thing they couldn't take away from me. It was my place of refuge, the spot from whence I could launch myself into the sweet dreams about Beulah and feats of greatness. No matter what happened to me, that old gunnysack would always be there to welcome me home.

I dragged myself toward the gas tanks, hoping with all my heart that Pete wouldn't see me. I'm never anxious to see Pete, but this time I was even less anxious than usual.

Luck was with me for a change, and Pete did not appear.

At last I could see it: my gunnysack, my friend.

It was waiting for me, calling my name, ready to embrace the folds of my tired and worn body, ready to launch me into . . .

A cat in my bed?

A grinning face with partially hooded eyes rose from my gunnysack. "Mmmmm, it's Hankie the Cowdog, and isn't this a wonderful coincidence!"

I summoned up just enough energy to issue a short growl. "Out of my bed, cat, before I . . ."

"Ah, ah, ah. Don't say anything you'll regret, Hankie. You haven't forgotten our little wager, have you?"

"I, uh . . . did I think to mention that, down deep in my heart, I don't approve of betting or wagering or gambling of any kind? I mean, I might have forgotten to . . ."

"You forgot to mention that, Hankie."

"Yes, well, it just slipped my . . ."

"It must have slipped your mind, Hankie."

"Exactly, and I'm sure the same thing has happened to you a time or two, you get caught up in something, excited and so forth, and before you realize it . . ."

"You've made a stupid mistake, hmmm?"

"Right. Well, stupid is pretty harsh . . ."

"A dumb mistake?"

"Yes, right, exactly. A dumb mistake. Or call it

40

a hasty decision, or it could be that you misunder-stood my true meaning, see, and you might have thought that I was making a foolish wager..."

"Um-hmmm, I did, Hankie, I certainly did."

"... when in fact the record will show that I was ... only words. Really. Honest."

Pete stretched out on my gunnysack and made himself right at home. I could hear him purring. Oh, and that tail of his was sticking straight up in the air.

"Mmmm, so you're saying that you didn't intend to make the bet, is that right, Hankie?"

"Right. Yes, and I'll be the first to admit it, Pete. I was misquoted and I'll have to take full responsibility for my actions. If I hadn't opened my big mouth, I never would have been misquoted in the first place."

"Um-hmmm."

"And as far as I'm concerned, we can chalk the whole thing up to experience. I mean, it's been a painful lesson for me, and why are you shaking your head?"

"No deal, Hankie."

"By 'no deal' do you mean ... no deal?"

"I mean, Hankie, that we made a bet and you lost."

"Oh, I see, yes, well, let me hasten to ..."

"And I'm ready to collect, Hankie."

"Huh? Collect? You mean . . . now wait a minute, Pete, you can't do this to me."

"Fair is fair, Hankie."

"I know that fair is fair, I've said that many times myself, but YOU CAN'T DO THIS TO ME!"

He grinned and purred and flicked his tail back and forth.

"Oh yes I can, Hankie. I won. You lost. I'm ready for you to pronounce me Head of Ranch Security."

"I won't! I can't! I . . ." I began pacing. "Listen, Pete, we can cut a deal, just you and me, right now. How about this: you'll be my First Assistant. Hey, wouldn't that be great?"

"Mmmm, and what about Drover?"

"Ha! He's out, through, finished, fired. It's just me and you, Pete, just the two of us, a team for the future!"

"No thank you."

"Huh? Okay, listen to this. Dog food, all you can eat for three days!"

"I'll pass on the dog food, Hankie."

"Good thinking, pal, I don't blame you, but here comes the killer deal of the century." I winked and leaned forward. "Bones, Pete. You give me a number and I'll deliver the goods."

He yawned, "I don't think so, Hankie, because bones hurt my teeth."

"Good point, hadn't thought of that, okay, we'll dig a little deeper in the old . . ."

"Hankie, had you thought of *begging* for your job?"

"Huh? Begging? Well, I . . . no, actually I hadn't thought of . . . begging. It sort of goes against my grains. Don't you see."

"Well, you might try it and see what happens." He studied his claws. "I've never been tested before, and who knows? It just might be my weak spot."

"I see. Begging. Could you give me some odds and percentages? I mean, I wouldn't want to go into a begging situation without knowing the . . . I'm sure you understand."

"Mmmm, yes, I understand, Hankie."

"I mean, it would be very painful."

"Oh, I know, it would hurt so bad!"

"Right, which is why I'd like to know . . ."

"Fifty-fifty."

"Fifty-fifty, which is only slightly better than average."

"That's the best I can offer, Hankie."

"Okay, well, fifty-fifty beats forty-forty, and uh . . . you said beg?"

"Umm-hmmm. Just hop on your back legs and beg, and we'll see what happens."

I coughed and cleared my throat, paced back and forth, scratched my ear, paced some more, and wrestled with this heavy decision.

"This is very difficult for me, Pete, I hope you understand that, and I mean VERY difficult and painful, but if this is what it takes to . . . I don't look forward to this, Pete. It's going to be very humiliating and I've never . . ."

"My patience is wearing thin, Hankie."

"Right, okay, and so the best thing for me to do is just . . . only for you would I do this, Pete, so watch carefully."

Against all my cowdog instincts, I hopped up on my back legs and brought my front paws into the Begging Position.

"There we go! What do you think of this, Pete?"

His smile went sour. "Mmmm, something's missing, Hankie. It just doesn't move me."

"Okay, what's missing is this little flourish which we call Moving the Paws While Begging. You'll love it, Pete, it's going to knock your socks off. Watch close!"

I did the maneuver, which is very difficult, by the way, and very few of your ordinary dogs have the muscle tone and coordination to pull it off.

"There you are, Pete, that's the whole show. Pretty impressive, huh? You ever see anything quite . . . you're shaking your head again, Pete, and I'm wondering what that means."

"Oh, Hankie, I'm afraid it didn't work, and just drat the luck!"

"Drat the . . . didn't . . . wait a minute. Are you saying that you're not going to call off the bet? After I lowered myself and humbled myself and made myself look like an idiot?"

The grin spread all the way across his mouth and his eyes brightened. "Mmmm yes, I'm afraid so, Hankie, but nice try anyway. Now, you may pronounce me Head of Ranch Security."

At last the pieces of the puzzle began falling into place. I had been duped and humiliated, and now I was fixing to be stripped of my rank.

I lowered my front paws to the ground and glared at him. "I should have known better than to do business with a cat." He nodded his head. "You'll regret this, Pete."

"Fair is fair, Hankie."

I took a gulp of air and plunged into the terrible unknown. "Very well. I pronounce you Head of Ranch Security, and I hope you get a big ringworm right where you sit down."

"Thank you, Hankie. Your unhappiness means

more to me than I can possibly express."

"Fine. Now get out of my bed."

"Ah, ah, ah! MY bed. It goes with the job."

My mind was reeling, my head was pounding, my body was begging for rest. I didn't have the energy to argue.

"All right, Pete. You've got it all: my job, my pride, and now my bed. You win. I'm whipped. The ranch is yours."

And with that, I turned and limped away from my bedroom, my home, and the gunnysack that had been my last friend in the world.

CHAPTER SIX

The Case of the Disheartened Chicken

I dragged myself up to the machine shed. Drover was there, sleeping on the cement pad in front of the big double doors.

I needed a friend to talk to, fellers, I mean I was at the bottom of my luck. On another occasion, I might have chosen a friend with more wealth, influence, and brains than Mister Stub-Tail, but this wasn't another occasion.

Yes, Drover had his flaws and his short-comings, but after working beside the little mutt for years, I knew in my heart that if he were the only dog available, I would choose him to be my best friend.

48

This was his lucky day.

"Drover, I don't want to alarm you, but the very worst thing that could possibly happen has just happened."

"Skonk snort zzzzzzzzzzzzz."

"Please don't panic. Screaming and running in circles won't help the situation."

"Snork glorg rumple ricky tattoo."

"I've come to inform you that I have gambled away my future and ruined my life. I'll be leaving soon to spend the rest of my miserable years living in ditches and gutters. I know this must come as a terrible shock."

"Skaw shurtling snort zzzzzzz."

"All I ask is that . . . wake up, you idiot! Can't you see that I'm pouring out my heart to you?"

He raised up and stared at me. His eyes were crossed, his ears were on crooked, and his tongue was hanging out the left side of his mouth.

"Oh my gosh, who's going to clean up all the blood?"

"Blood? What blood?"

He staggered to his feet. "I can't stand the sight of blood, where am I?" His eyes began to focus. "Oh, hi Hank, I must have dozed off. Did you hear about the murder?"

"Murder? No, what happened?"

"Gosh, I'm not sure, I just heard about it, but somebody got murdered, maybe it was a chicken, and they busted into the chicken house and cut her heart out and chopped it up into little pieces!"

"Chopped up her heart!"

"Yeah, it was awful. And then they poured out the pieces of heart all over the ground! And then they chopped up her lizzard and giver and . . ."

"Hold it. Do you mean gizzard and liver?"

"Yeah, did you hear about it too? Oh my gosh, I guess it's true, Hank, and there was blood everywhere, I saw it with my own eyes!"

"You witnessed this unspeakable murder with your own eyes?"

"I think they were mine. Yeah, they must have been."

"Holy smokes, Drover, why wasn't I informed?"

"Well, I never would have thought you'd be interested."

I glared at him. "You didn't think I'd be interested in a ghastly murder?"

"No, I meant my eyes."

"I don't care about your eyes!"

"That's why I didn't tell you."

"I'm talking about the . . ." Then I remembered. "But never mind all that, Drover. I've just lost my post, so it doesn't matter anyway."

"Well, there's a whole bunch of them over in the post pile, and I think there's a rabbit over there too."

"Don't mention that word in my presence, Drover."

"You mean post?"

"No, I mean rabbit. A rabbit has just ruined my life."

"I'll be derned."

"Because of that lying, cheating rabbit, I have lost my post."

"Ate the whole thing, huh?"

"Exactly, and I'd appreciate it if you'd never speak of rabbits again."

"I guess they'll eat anything."

"It just breaks my heart to think about this terrible loss."

"Oh, you can always find another post. Digging the hole's the big problem."

"Yes, it's an enormous hole, Drover, and I'm wondering if I'll ever be able to fill it."

"Well, you might try dirt. That works sometimes."

"A whole lifetime down the drain, Drover, and I have no one to blame but myself."

"I'd blame the cowboys."

"No, it was my fault. All the cowboys did was laugh at my stupidity."

"Yeah, but if they'd feed these rabbits once in a while, maybe they wouldn't have to eat fence posts."

My eyes swung around and focused on him. "WHAT?"

"I said . . . well, let's see, what did I say? I think I've already forgot."

"Out with it! Something about fence posts."

"Oh yeah. I said, if they'd feed these fence posts once in a while, they wouldn't have to eat so many rabbits."

"The cowboys are eating rabbits?"

"No, the fence posts."

"The cowboys are eating fence posts?"

"No, the fence posts are eating . . . you said the rabbits were eating . . . fence posts?"

I looked into the huge emptiness of his eyes. "Drover, has it ever occurred to you that you might be going insane?"

"I've wondered about that."

"It has already happened. The post to which I was referring was not a fence post, but rather my post as Head of Ranch Security."

"I'll be derned."

"I lost it in a bet with the cat. I bet Pete that I could catch the Lumber-Pile Bunny and I failed. Which means that Pete is now Head of

Ranch Security and I am Head of the Broken Heart Society."

"Yeah, but the chicken doesn't have a heart at all."

"It was a rabbit, and yes, he was utterly heartless."

"No, I mean the chicken that was murdered and disheartened."

"Oh yes, I'd almost forgotten that. You witnessed the crime yourself?"

"I think it was me."

I looked up at the sky and heaved a sigh. "Drover, there was a time, not so very long ago, when the mention of such a crime would have gotten my full attention. I would have jumped right into the middle of the case and begun a thorough investigation.

"But now, because of my own foolish mistakes, I've lost my job and therefore my authority to press an investigation. I suggest you take your repeat to Port . . . your report to Pete, that is, and let him handle it. He's in charge now."

"Oh my gosh!"

"Well said, Drover. I think we both know what'll come of this."

"Yeah, the chicken'll never get her heart back and the ranch'll go to pot."

"Exactly. But it can't be helped, Drover. I'm afraid that I'm leaving this old ranch in quite a mess."

"Leaving!"

"Yes, Drover, I'm leaving. There's nothing left for me here except the sad memory of how things used to be, and that is nothing but a sad memory. I have failed my ranch, my hundreds of friends, my profession, myself. I'll spend the rest of my days wandering Life's ditches and gutters—a dog without a home."

"Boy, that's tough," he said, as he gnawed at a flea on his left flank. "If you put your job up in that bet, what did Pete put up against it?"

"I . . . that's a foolish question, Drover. Obviously, since I risked something dear and precious to me, the cat put up something of equal worth."

"Yeah, but he doesn't have anything of equal worth."

"Of course he does."

"Such as?"

"Such as . . . well, he . . . that is . . . what are you driving at, Drover? Are you suggesting that I might have been suckered into a stupid bet?"

"I wondered."

"Because if that's what you're suggesting, let me intrude into your little world of fantasy and

point out . . ." I began pacing, as I often do to stim-
ulate my thought processes. "Your whole house is
an argument of cards, Drover, and all I have to do
to send it tumbling down is to remove one single
card."

"Yeah, and I've got a feeling that it's a joker."

Suddenly I stopped pacing and whirled around.
"Because, Drover, there was a joker in the deck."

"I knew it."

"Don't you see what's happened here? It was a
rigged game, Drover, a phony bet, a put-up deal.
You thought Pete had won it fair and square, but
what you overlooked was the obvious fact that
HE CHEATED!"

"I think that's what I was driving at."

"Maybe you were droving, Driver, but you ran
out of gas before you solved the mystery."

"My name's Drover."

"Exactly. You were close, Drover, and I know
perfectly well what your name is and don't inter-
rupt my presentation again, but not close enough.
For you see, Pete risked nothing in our wager and
therefore the entire bet is cancelled. And as of
this moment, I am reclaiming my title as Head of
Ranch Security."

"Boy, that's a relief."

"Exactly. And my first action will be to throw

all units into the investigation of this gruesome murder you witnessed with your own eyes."

"Either that or I dreamed it."

"And my second action will be to settle all accounts with Pete the Barncat, who has become a minutes to society. Come on, Drover, to the chicken house!"

And with that, we went streaking to the chicken house to investigate one of the most chilling crimes I had encountered in my whole career.

CHAPTER SEVEN

Bloody Writing
on the Wall

W e reached the chicken house only seconds
after I had sounded the alarm.

The first thing we did upon reaching the scene
of the crime was to plow into the middle of seven
hens who were loitering outside. They were pecking around in the dirt and clucking to each other
and performing the usual absurd rituals you
expect to find among chickens, who are stupid
beyond belief.

Since they were blocking our path, we seized
the opportunity to mix pleasure with business. We
just by George bulldozed 'em and sent 'em squawk-
ing in all directions.

I love doing that.

We sent them pecking . . . eh, packing, that is,

and once again I experienced that feeling of exhilaration and well-being and mental health and so forth. That done, we plunged into the murder house and went to work.

As my eyes adjusted to the gloomy light, I did a visual sweep of the walls and ceiling, using my photogenic memory to record even the smallest details.

"Well, Drover, do you notice anything unusual?"

"Yeah, it stinks in here."

"Exactly. And does that tell you anything?"

"I'm glad we're not chickens."

I gave him a stern glare. "Let's not dwell upon the obvious. We're looking for clues, the tiny details that form the signature of the criminal."

"Well, let's see. Wait, hold it! What's that over there?"

I rushed "over there," following the angle of Drover's nose. It led me to the west wall, in the very gloomiest corner of the room. There, my eyes fell upon some mysterious form of writing.

"This is some mysterious form of writing, Drover."

"Yeah, and it's written in red! Could it be . . ."

"I'll take it from here Drover. Red writing. Does that ring any bells with you?"

He lifted one ear. "Not really."

"Here's a hint: Grandma's house."

"Uh . . . dinner bell?"

"Forget the bells, Drover, and concentrate on the hints. Here's another one: wolf."

"Arf?"

"No."

"Bow wow?"

"Wolf, the animal, a ferocious beast waiting to eat someone."

"Oh. Well, let's see here. What was the first thing you said?"

"Red writing."

The huge blank of his face suddenly filled with signs of recognition. "I've got it, I've got it! Little Red . . . oh my gosh, you don't think the killer was Little Red Writing Hood, do you?"

"Yes, Drover, either Little Write Redding Hood or someone in her disguise. She left a clue behind, as they always do, never dreaming that we would put 'red' and 'writing' together and come up with her true identity."

"What made her do such an awful thing?"

"We don't have the answer to that one yet, but I have an idea that it's just a matter of time until we come up with a motive."

"It makes me sad."

"Snap out of it, Drover, because there's still

more to come. The mysterious message was written in red, correct?"

"Yeah, I already said that."

"But I said it first."

"But I saw it first."

"But I entered the chicken house first."

"But I was the first one up this morning."

"Yes, Drover, but I never went to bed, so your claim to being the first one up just doesn't hold water."

Suddenly, his eyes popped open. "Oh my gosh, speaking of water, I've got to GO!"

"We're in the middle of a very important investigation."

"Yeah, but we're fixing to be in the middle of a flood." He was hopping up and down and biting his lip.

"Very well, Drover, you may be excused, but this will have to go into your record."

He scrambled out the door. I waited inside, tapping my toe and counting off the seconds. I hate wasting time. He returned moments later, wearing a big smile.

"I'm ready for anything now."

"Where were we?"

"Let's see. I was the first one up this morning."

"No, you weren't, and why were we talking about that in the first place?"

"Well, let's see." He thought. I waited. "I don't remember. Something about water."

"Yes, of course. Water is very important to all life on earth. Without water, there would be no watermelons and . . . I've lost my train of thought."

"I've always wanted to ride in a caboose."

"Wait, I've got it. We were discussing the mysterious red writing, and I was about to point out a very important detail that escaped your attention."

"You mean that it might have been written in blood?"

I narrowed my eyes and glared at the runt. "Who's in charge of this investigation, you or me?"

"Well, you, I guess."

"That's correct. I am in charge of the investigation, and if there are any new and startling revelations to be made, I will be the one to make them. Is that clear?"

"Okay, but I was the first one up this morning."

"Fine. You were the first one up, and now you will be the first one to shut your little trap while I reveal that this mysterious message on the wall *was probably written in BLOOD.*"

"Oh my gosh!"

"Yes indeed. Now we are only one step away from wrapping this case up. The only question left unanswered is, what does the mysterious message say?

"I will now move closer to the wall and try to uncrypt and decipher the message."

I moved closer to the wall and studied the message. It appeared to consist of a single word.

"All right, Drover, stand by. The first letter is A."

"Oh, that's awful!"

"The second letter appears to be an L."

"Okay, I got it, Hank. That makes A-L."

"Exactly. The third letter is F, followed by an R."

"A-L-F-R. That doesn't make any sense to me."

"Patience, son. The next letter is an E. And, stand by, the final letter is a D. There we are, Drover. Now read them all back to me."

"A-L-F-R-E-D."

"There must be some mistake. That doesn't spell Little Red Writing Hood."

"Maybe she couldn't spell."

"Very possible, Drover."

"Wait! It sounds kind of like . . . Alfred . . . doesn't it?"

"Alfred?"

"Little Alfred?"

"HUH?" I whirled around and took a closer look at the . . . "Drover, if you had studied the clues more carefully, you would have realized that this word was written in RED CRAYON, not blood."

"Oh my gosh, it's getting worse and worse! You think Little Alfred was the killer?"

"No."

"The chicken bled crayon instead of blood?"

"No."

"I'm all confused."

"Yes." I paced back and forth in front of him. "Drover, in your report of the ghastly murder, you mentioned that the killer had cut up the chicken's heart and poured the pieces out on the ground. Do you see any signs of a chicken heart?"

"Well . . . not really."

"Your report went on to say that 'blood was everywhere,' to use your exact words. Do you see any signs of blood?"

"Well . . ."

"There is no blood, Drover, and there are no pieces of a chicken's heart. That means there was no murder. It means that Little Alfred wrote his name on the chicken house wall with a red crayon. It means that you have led us on a fool's errand."

"Well, I'll be derned. I sure thought . . . you don't reckon I dreamed all that, do you?"

I stopped pacing and stabbed him with a gaze of solid steel. "I reckon you did, you dunce. I had just told you that I was pouring my heart out to you."

"Oh, is that what it was?"

"Yes. But instead of listening to a friend in need, you concocted an outrageous story about blood and murder."

"I knew it had something to do with hearts."

"Drover, you have just brought the Security Division to its lowest point in history. Do you realize that if someone had been watching us for the past half hour, he might very well think that we are a couple of fools?"

"Boy, that's wrong."

"Of course it is, but mere facts can lead to a false impression. Hence, you and I will take a vow of secrecy and swear never to reveal the deep, dark stupidity of what we've just done."

"My lips are sealed."

I put my paw on his shoulder. "And remember, Drover. Even though it's unpleasant to lie and cover up, we're doing this for our own good."

"Yeah, and somebody had to do it."

"Exactly. Now we will sneak out of here and forget this ever happened and hope that no one was watching."

And with that, we backed out the door and erased the entire incident from the memory of the world.

(NOTE: At this point in the story, I would appreciate it if you would remove this chapter from your book, since it contains very sensitive information that could damage the future work of the Security Division. Thanks.)

The Healing Waters
of Emerald Pond

Once outside the chicken house, we made some fast tracks and got the heck away from there.

It had suddenly occurred to me that if Sally May saw me coming out of the chicken house, or even standing close to it, she might leap to some false conclusions.

I mean, on more than one occasion she had accused me of committing unthinkable crimes, against her chickens—such as eating them and/or their eggs.

Crazy, huh? It's common knowledge that cow-dogs, and especially Heads of Ranch Security, NEVER eat chickens or suck eggs. I mean, we protect the stupid birds and their equally stupid eggs, so it would make no sense at all for us to turn right around and eat them—although I must admit that . . . hmm.

What I mean is that all charges against me had been false and outrageous and unfair and unfoundered, but in the Security Business we must guard ourselves against even the slightest appearance of naughty behavior.

And fellers, two dogs backing out of the chicken house in the middle of a normal work day might have been . . . I think you get the point. And so did I, which explains why I got away from there just as fast as I could travel.

Well, we had dodged that particular bullet and made our way down to Emerald Pond— my own private name, by the way, for one of my very favorite spots on the ranch, the lovely green pool of water formed by the overflow of the septic tank.

That investigation of the chicken house had pretty muchly worn me out and I still had a slight headache from my encounter with the corral fence and I was ready to dive into the warm embrace, so to speak, of Emerald Pond, whose waters are known to have curative and healing powers.

I can also reveal that those same green

waters can provide a dog with a very impressive "calling card," you might say—a deep manly aroma that has been known to steal the hearts of the ladies and just by George sweep them off their feet.

Pretty impressive, huh? And it's MY pond.

Well, I sprang right into the middle of Emerald Pond, filled my nostrils with its sweet perfume, rolled around, kicked my legs in the air, climbed out, and gave myself a good shake.

Say, that little dip had left me feeling like a million bucks!

Drover had watched all this from dry land.

"Son, one of these days you're going to realize what you've been missing."

"Yeah, I know. But I don't like water."

"This isn't just water. It's tonic, a magic elixir that's full of vitamins and minerals. I'd almost be willing to bet that if you stuck your stub tail into these waters, it would grow out to normal size."

"No fooling?"

"Yup. It's powerful stuff."

"But I kind of like my tail the way it is."

"Well, to each his own, Drover. If you're happy with a chopped-off, deformed stub, I guess that's all that matters."

"I never thought of it as deformed."

"Then forget I said anything about it."

"Okay."

"Your happiness is the most important thing."

"Thanks, Hank."

"And the fact that everyone else laughs at your ridiculous tail is irrevelent. Irreverent. Irreffluent."

"Irrelevant?"

"I'll speak for myself, Drover, but thanks anyway. The word is IRREFFLUENT."

"Okay. But do you really think my tail's deformed?"

I sat down and scratched a troublesome spot just behind my left ear. "Are you asking for an honest answer or one that sugarcoats the truth?"

"Whichever one makes my tail look better."

"All right, you have a magnificent stub of a tail."

"You're just saying that so I won't think it's deformed!"

"That's what you wanted, wasn't it?"

"No," he began to sniffle and cry, "I want a tail that the other dogs won't laugh at! All my life I've wanted a tail that wasn't handicapped! How can I ever find happiness with a deformed tail?"

"That's a tough question, son."

"I'm so miserable and unhappy! I hate my tail! Why can't I have a normal tail like a normal dog? All I ever wanted to be was normal."

"Drover, your tail can be fixed."

"You really think so? You mean there's hope?"

"Son, the cure for your condition has been right here all along. You just haven't used it."

"You mean . . ."

"Exactly. You must sit in Emerald Pond for two hours."

"That's all?"

"Sit with your tail under the healing waters for two hours and repeat these words over and over."

"What words?"

"I haven't said them yet."

"Oh."

"'Lizards, spiders, warts and scales,
    Give this dog a normal tail.'"

A smile bloomed on his face. "I think I can do it, Hank, and boy howdy, I'm sure excited!"

"I'm happy for you, Drover. If you follow those directions to the letter, I can almost guarantee that you'll come out with a normal tail."

His smile slipped. "What's an 'almost guarantee'?"

"I, uh . . . it's just one peg below a Gold Plated Guarantee."

"I'd rather have the Gold Plated, if it's okay."

"We're out of those, Drover."

"Oh rats."

I stood up and stretched. "So get your little fanny into the water and begin your therapy. I'll be back in a couple of hours to check things out."

"Where you going?"

I couldn't help smirking. "If you recall, Drover, I have a little score to settle with the cat. While your tail is growing, Pete's tail just might get shortened by a few inches," I gave him a wink, "if you know what I mean."

"Something's wrong with your eye."

"What?"

"I said, THERE'S SOMETHING WRONG WITH YOUR EYE!"

"Don't yell at me, there's nothing wrong with my ears!"

"I know. It's your eye."

"What are you talking about?"

"Your eye was twitching. I saw it myself."

I positioned my nose right in front of his face. "I was winking, you brick, to show that I had let you in on a little secret."

"Oh. Well, I'll be derned. I thought . . ."

"Yes, I heard what you thought, and it's obvious that sharing my secret with you was a waste of time. I'm sorry I bothered."

"That's okay, you couldn't help it."

"Thanks."

"You're welcome, and I hope it gets better."

"What?"

"Your eye."

"Drover?"

"What?"

"HUSH."

I left the runt sitting in Emerald Pond and went looking for the cat. My first stop was the gas tanks, to see if Pete was still occupying my gunnysack bed. Much to my disappointment, he had left.

So I went padding up to the yard gate to check out his usual loafing spots, the main one being right beside the back door where he often lolled around in the shade, waiting for someone to come outside. Any time the door opened, you see, he would try to weasel his way into the house.

That's a cat for you, always trying to weasel his way into something or other.

I didn't see him on the back step and was about to check out the machine shed when I heard a voice that caused my bodily parts to freeze in place and the hair to rise on my back.

It was the cat. "Mmmm, hello, Hankie. I bet you wish you were still Head of Ranch Security."

Ho ho! Kitty-Kitty had just set himself up for a rude surprise.

CHAPTER NINE

Pete's Mindless Senseless Vandalism of a Sheet

That voice does something to me, causes my hair to rise and my ears to jump to the Full Alert position.

A growl begins to rumble in my throat, my eyes narrow to slits and my lips begin to twitch and my teeth expose themselves in all their frightening glory.

I turned toward the sound of the voice and saw him, sitting beneath the clothesline and looking up at a clean sheet that was flapping in the wind. Now and then he would lift his front paw and bat the sheet.

"Did you just say something, cat?"

"Mmm-hmmm. I said, I'll bet you wish you were still Head of Ranch Security."

"Is that what you bet? Well, this is turning out to be a bad day for your bets, Kitty. I don't wish I was still Head of Ranch Security, because I AM Head of Ranch Security."

He turned his head around and smirked at me. "No you're not. You lost your job in a gambling accident."

"Ha, ha, ha. Ho, ho, ho. Hee, hee, hee. You make me laugh, Pete. And lest you get the wrong impression, let me emphasize that I'm laughing at YOU."

"Mmm, isn't that interesting." He slapped at the sheet. "I'm the new Head of Ranch Security and you don't have a job, but you're laughing at me? That's very interesting, Hankie."

I marched down the fence. "I can see that you still haven't figgered it out, cat. I have cancelled that bet."

"You can't cancel what's already happened, Hankie. Even you should know that."

"I have cancelled the bet. It's off, it's over, it's suspended, it's null and void. It's history and it never happened."

"Mmmm! It's history and it never happened. What an interesting idea."

"That's correct, Kitty. On this ranch, history is whatever I say it is."

"But you're forgetting one small detail, Hankie." He hit the switchblade in his paw and his claws suddenly appeared. He admired them while he spoke. "Your bet was backed up by your Solemn Cowdog Oath. You can't take that back."

"Oh yeah? I'm afraid you overlooked one small detail, kitty. The Solemn Cowdog Oath doesn't apply to cheating situations or crooked deals. You see, I analyzed our wager and found that we were both betting on the same thing: my job."

He fluttered his eyelids. "That seems fair."

"That seems *crooked,* and you know it. You almost pulled it off, Pete, but I'm afraid you've been caught in the web of your own spider."

"You're so clever, Hankie." He yawned and came slinking over to the fence. He sat down, stared at me with his big cat eyes, and began twitching the end of his tail. "If you'll lean a little closer to the fence, I'll tell you a secret."

I caught myself just in time and pulled my face away. "Lean closer to the fence, so that you can slap me across the nose with your claws? As you've done before on several occasions? Sorry, Pete, your sneaky tricks are getting threadbare. That one isn't going to fly."

He glared at me. Then he drew himself up, threw an arch in his back, and hissed at me. Before I knew it, a ferocious growl was thundering in my throat and I was seized by a powerful instinct to destroy the fence between us.

But iron discipline saved me just in time. I sat down and laughed at him.

"I guess you thought you could hiss and throw me into a frenzy of irrational behavior, right? Then I'd tear down the fence between us and chase you around the yard, right? And then Sally May would come running to save you, and I'd get pounded with the broom, right?"

He glared daggers at me through the fence.

"Sorry, Pete. I've made a few mistakes in the past, but it happens that I learn from my mistakes. Your cheap tricks just aren't working anymore. Sorry."

Oh, you should have seen his icy glare when I told him that! It killed him, just by George ruined his day.

By this time his ears were pinned down on his head and the pupils of his eyes had grown to the size of quarters. "You're making me angry, Hankie, and when I get angry it makes me want to use my claws and tear something up."

"Oh yeah? Well, if it gets too overwhelming for

you, Kitty, I'll be glad to meet you down along the creek, but if you think I'm going to get suckered into a fight on Sally May's doorstep, you're very muchly mistaken."

"I'm getting angrier and angrier."

"And I'm loving every second of it, Pete. Keep it up. Here, try this on for size." I stuck my tongue out at him.

"I can't control myself much longer, Hankie."

"Oh, yeah? Well, see how you like this." I crossed my eyes AND stuck out my tongue, all at the same time, see, and oh my, that really ripped him.

He was yowling now, the way cats do when they're so mad they could spit, only they can't spit so they yowl. "Just for that, I'm going to tear up a sheet!"

"Oh really? Tear up one of Sally May's clean sheets? You'd better not."

"I will, you'll see!"

And with that, the stupid cat dashed back to the clothesline and climbed the sheet. I could hear his claws ripping into the cloth.

"UMMMMMMMMMMMMM!! You're ripping the sheet!"

"I don't even care, it's all your fault, you've made me so angry I just can't control myself!"

Well, as you might imagine, I was almost beside

myself with joy and happiness. At last I had pushed Pete over the edge of the brink. Now all I had to do was sound the alarm, alert Sally May to what her precious kitty was doing, and then sit back to watch the fur fly.

I barked the alarm. "Attention please! Hank calling Sally May, come in Sally May. Red Alert at the clothesline, repeat Red Alert at the clothesline! We have spotted a deranged cat who is destroying one of your clean sheets. Report to the clothesline at once, and bring broom."

That would do it.

I sat back and prepared to enjoy the show. In a matter of seconds, Sally May would come flying out that door—her eyes filled with sheer meanness and . . .

I kept waiting. I frowned and began pacing. My eyes were riveted on the screen door. The seconds passed. No sign of Sally May.

That was odd.

And in the meantime, Kitty continued to climb the sheet and perform mindless acts of vandalism. Mindless vandalism has always bothered me. I mean, there's no reason for it. It's just . . .

Still no sign of Sally May. Could she have gone to town? No, but she might have been taking a bath, in which case . . .

Senseless destruction of ranch property—that's what I was forced to watch, and before I knew it, a ferocious growl was thundering in my throat and I was seized by a powerful instinct to destroy the fence between us.

But, of course, this was Sally May's deal, not . . .

My hair began to rise and my ears jumped to the Full Alert position. My eyes narrowed to slits and my lips began to twitch and my teeth exposed themselves in all their frightening glory.

I heard a loud R-I-P! This was intolerable, unbearable. How much longer could I sit there, an idle speculator to mindless vandalism and the senseless destruction of ranch property? At what point did an idle speculator become a part of the crime?

I mean, there's such a thing as moral outrage. Some dogs have it and some dogs don't, and those of us who . . .

All at once I was finding it very hard to . . . that cat was not only defacing Sally May's sheet, but in a deeper sense he was committing a senseless act of senseless vandalism against MY RANCH!

Well, you know me. I take that stuff pretty serious. Nobody messes with my . . .

Okay, that was it.

Red Alert, full throttle, all systems go, open fire, launch all torpedoes, charge, bonzai! THIS WAS WAR!!

I leaped over the fence like a buck deer, crossed the yard with three huge leaps, and flew right into the middle of that sheet, wrapped up old Pete in a nice little package, and was well on my way to . . . screen door?

Ah ha, Sally May had finally answered the call and was coming to the rescue. And yes, her eyes were flaming and smoke was curling out of her nostrils and she was definitely armed with the broom, and I could see that she was ready to do some serious damage to her precious, perfect, sniveling little weasel of a cat.

I sat up straight, held my head at a proud angle, and wagged my tail as if to say, "Welcome to the war, Sally May. As you can see, I have just arrested this . . .

HUH?

He'd been right there in the sheet.

Just moments before.

Wrapped up in a nice little package from which he couldn't possibly . . .

Sally May was standing over me. She looked very angry, very angry indeed. I began to develop a funny feeling about this deal.

I lifted my eyes and tried to smile and, uh, thumped my tail on the, uh, ground.

"Uh, Sally May," I tried to say, "I think I can explain everything."

"You nasty dog, you've ruined my sheet!"

"Me? No, it was the ..." WHAP! "... cat, don't you see, I caught Pete ..." WHAP! "... honest, no kidding, I'm being very serious about ..." WHAP!

"You get out of my yard and don't you ever come back!"

I never argue with a loaded broom. I ran in a tight circle for a moment, dodging that deadly killer broom, and then broke away and went zooming toward the machine shed . . .

. . . forgetting for the moment that the fence was still there, which caused a slight pile-up beside the foot scraper and actually hurt worse than the broom itself, but eventually we . . .

I ran for my life and hid in the darkest corner of the machine shed. It was there that I straightened my neck and licked my wounds.

And began plotting my final revenge against the cat.

CHAPTER TEN

The Infamous Black Hole of Mustard

I just didn't understand.

Everything had been going my way. I had sniffed out all of Pete's sneaky tricks and had made the appropriate countermoves. I had held my temper, resisted the temptation to make hash of him, had maintained Iron Discipline throughout.

I had even laughed at him.

I had known from the start what he was trying to do, and yet he had somehow managed to do it anyway.

How could one cat be so lucky, so often?

It strained my concept of luck. It strained my concept of who I was and who I had always wanted to be. It strained my . . .

My eyes were rolling around in circles and,

hmmm, I appeared to be banging my head against the northwest leg of the workbench.

Something bad was happening to me, fellers. I was losing control of my control. My instruments were shorting out. I felt myself spiraling toward the Infamous Black Hole of Mustard.

In one last desperate effort to save myself, I took a firm grip on the cement floor with all four paws and fought against the tremendous swirling vacuum sweeper that threatened to swallow me up.

And—you won't believe this—I saved myself from vacuumization by singing a song. Why not? "Music hath charms to soothe the savage beast," says the old saying, and here's how the song went:

I Must Dispose of the Cat

I don't understand what's going on here.
It makes me have questions about my career.
I used to have pride, I thought I was shrewd,
So how come my game plan is coming
    unglued?

My countermoves backfire, my plots go awry,
I've got indigestion from Pete's humble pie.
It's happened so often, I'm starting to think
This cat will eventually drive me to drink

So to save the dignity of my ranch,
To stop this mental avalanche
I hereby burn the olive branch.
I must dispose of the cat!

It's not that I'm bitter or violent or mean.
I'm not in the habit of making a scene.
I don't take positions from which I won't
   budge,
Yet now I perceive that I'm holding a grudge.

There's nothing too personal in this,
   I submit.
Well, maybe I'm bothered by cats, I admit,
Their hissing and yowling and humping
   their backs.
I hate them, that's all, it's as simple as that.

So to save the dignity of my ranch,
To stop this mental avalanche
I hereby burn the olive branch.
I must dispose of the cat!

El Gato is rumored to have several lives,
Nine, I believe, which is four more than five.
But gato and gravy, served up on a plate
Will get the grand total down closer to eight.

A kitty for supper, a kitty for lunch,
A kitty *con queso,* a kitty with punch.
A kitty for snacks, oh my this is fun!
And shortly the total will shrink down
    to none.

    So to save the dignity of my ranch,
    To stop this mental avalanche
    I hereby burn the olive branch.
    I must consider the pros and cons
    Of bumping off the cat!

When I had finished the song, I looked around.
I was standing in the middle of the machine shed.
The bells and whistles had vanished. My mind had
cleared.

Best of all, the Infamous Black Hole of Mustard
had swallowed itself and returned to the ethers of
the vapor, or wherever it is that Black Holes come
from.

But the important thing was that I had
snatched myself back from the edge of despair and
had survived one of the most dangerous moments
of my career.

And, all at once, it was clear what I had to do.
Heh, heh. Oh, a few details still had to be worked
out, but those were small matters of procedure.

I wondered why I hadn't thought of this sooner. Surely it was a testimony to my sweet nature and gentle disposition—and yes, to a certain dread of consequences. Sally May, for example.

I had a suspicion that she would not think kindly of my plots and schemes, and that fact pretty muchly determined the method I finally chose for the job.

Here's what I did. I left the machine shed and, on silent feet, went hunting for the villain. I checked out the yard. He wasn't there, which was good. I checked those tall weeds around the water well, and he wasn't there too.

I was on my way down to the corrals when I happened to glance to my left and saw something that brought bubbles of joy bubbling to the surface of my . . . something. *Pete was asleep on my gunnysack bed beneath the gas tanks.*

This cat, who had been so cunning and shrewd only hours before, had made the incredibly dumb mistake of taking an afternoon nap—away from the house and on my bed! He was making it easy for me, which I appreciated.

There are several ways of catnapping a kid . . . kidnapping a cat, I should say, and also several ways of getting your eyebrows torn off your face by a hissing, spitting, clawing little buzz saw—unless you happen to pick the cat up by the loose skin behind his neck, in which case he will hang as limp as a sock.

You see, I had watched Little Alfred in action on many occasions and had observed him dragging Pete all over the ranch in this manner.

Pete never suspected a thing. I slipped up to the gas tanks, scooped him up in my jaws, and was well on my way to the wild canyon country north of headquarters before he knew what was happening.

"Mmmm, you're taking me somewhere, Hankie." I couldn't respond because my mouth was full of cat, don't you see, and I didn't have anything to say to him anyway. "It's a nice evening for a walk in the pasture, Hankie, but I think we've gone far enough."

Silence.

"Hankie, I'm wondering where we're going. Are you listening?"

I was listening but my heart had turned to cement. I continued on a northward course until I reached the base of the caprock. There, I stopped and released the cat.

"Here we are, kitty. This is where you get off. It's called Coyote City."

Pete had his ears pinned back. He humped up

his back and hissed at me, also took a swipe at me with his paw but I managed to dodge it.

"You know, cat, if you'd ever shown any signs of wanting to get along with me, things never would have gotten to this point. But you're so greedy and spiteful, you've forced me to take drastic measures."

He yowled and hissed.

"You've driven me to this. What happens is your own fault."

He yowled and hissed.

"Nobody ever deserved this more than you, Pete, but on second thought it does seem a little severe, and if you approached me just right, I might consider accepting an apology."

"I'll give you an apology, Hankie. Just take two steps this way and I'll give you an apology you'll never forget."

"There, you see? You cats won't compromise. You don't even try to get along. But after considering the finality of what we're doing here, I'm willing to give you one last chance to apologize and start all over with a clean slate."

"Cats don't compromise, Hankie, and we don't ever apologize for anything. If we can't run the show, we don't play."

I shook my head. "Hey Pete, you might think we're playing games here, but let me point out that when I leave, you're going to be all alone in the middle of coyote country."

He continued to glare at me. "Cats enjoy being alone, Hankie, because when we're by ourselves, we're in the very best of company."

This was hopeless! I began pacing. "Listen, cat, you don't know what you're talking about. Maybe you've never had any experience with coyotes but I have, and I can tell you that their very favorite meal is fresh cat. Now, if you'll just..."

"I can take care of myself, Hankie. I don't need the help of a bungling dog."

I stopped pacing and our glares met. "Okay, Pete, let's lay all the cards on the table. I brought you up here because I wanted to bump you off. Now that we're here, I find myself having second thoughts about it. If you'll just make a small apology..."

"Not interested, Hankie."

"Okay. If you'll promise to make a small apology within the next three days..."

"Apology is a word cats don't understand, Hankie."

"All right, this is absolutely your last chance. If you'll promise *to consider thinking about* making a small apology..."

He grinned and shook his head.

"Very well, Pete, in that case I have no choice but to order you to return to the ranch with me—immediately. And that's a direct order."

"But Hankie, I don't take orders—not from you, not from anyone. Cats are very independent and we take care of ourselves."

"Will you listen to reason?" I yelled at him. "This place is crawling with wild hungry coyotes. If I leave you here, you won't have a chance to take care of yourself because you'll be a kitty sandwich."

He studied his claws. "I'll go back with you, Hankie."

"That's better."

"IF you'll make a full and complete apology to me, and IF you'll agree to let me be Head of Ranch Security forever and ever."

HUH?

I stared at him. "Are you crazy? You want me to . . . okay, fine, I should have known better than to talk sense to a cat. Have it your way, Pete, I'm washing my paws of the whole mess. Good-bye and good riddance!"

And with that, I whirled around and headed back to headquarters, satisfied that I had done the world a tremendous service.

CHAPTER ELEVEN

Total Happiness
Without Pete

Trotting back to headquarters, I felt great.
Wonderful. Tremendous. At last, peace and
quiet. At last, total happiness. At last . . .

The dumb cat! How could he . . . can you imagine him thinking that he could . . . well, that was
just fine, everything had turned out for the . . . and
furthermore, I didn't give a rip.

And even if I did give a rip, it was a very small
rip.

I put it out of my mind, just by George wiped
it out of my memory and forgot that I had . . .
never mind.

I made it back to headquarters an hour or so
before sundown and headed straight to Emerald
Pond. It was time to check up on Mister Stub-Tail.

Sure enough, there he was, sitting in the water and looking up at the clouds. I was glad to have something to take my mind off of . . . well, other matters, shall we say.

"All right, Drover, you can come out of the water now."

"Hank, did you hear the news? Pete's gone! They can't find him anywhere."

"Oh really? My goodness, that's . . ."

"Sally May and Little Alfred looked all over for him. I'm kind of worried."

"Worry about growing a new tail, Drover, and leave the cats to take care of themselves."

"Yeah, but what if he wanders away and the coyotes get him?"

I put my nose in his face. "I don't want to talk about cats or think about cats, do you understand?"

"Gosh, you're kind of touchy."

"I'm not touchy! The subject bores me, that's all."

"You didn't see Pete while you were gone, did you?"

"I, uh, no, of course not, and why would you ask such a ridiculous question?"

"Just wondered. Where'd you go?"

"I went for a little walk, Pete."

"I'm Drover. You called me Pete."

"Yes, of course, how silly of me. I went for a walk."

He looked at me and twisted his head to the side. "You're acting kind of funny. Is anything wrong?"

"Wrong? Why, heavens no. Everything's great. Wonderful. Terrific. Now get your little self out of the water, Pete, and let's take a look at your tail."

"You just called me Pete again."

"Get out of the water!"

"Gosh, you don't have to yell and scream."

"I'M NOT YELLING AND SCREAMING!!!"

"You are too yelling and screaming, and I don't understand why you're acting so funny all of a sudden, and my tail didn't grow one little bit."

"How do you know that?"

"Well . . . I checked on it . . . a couple of times."

"*You checked on it!* You mean, you got up out of the water?"

"Yeah, I got bored. And tired of sitting."

"What about the magic words? Did you say the magic words over and over for two solid hours?"

"Well . . . they weren't very solid."

"What are you saying?"

"Well . . . I forgot the words after a while, and they were kind of boring too."

I shook my head. "I should have known. Well, stand up and let's have a look. I hope that your foolish behavior didn't cause a reversal of the growing process."

His eyes flew open. "A reversal! You mean . . ."

"Exactly. Sometimes when you fool around with powerful medicine, it has bad side effects. It's possible, Pete, that you might have no tail at all."

"Oh my gosh! What would everyone say?"

"They'd point at you and laugh and call you Little Mister Lost-His-Tail."

"Don't say that, Hank! I don't think I could stand it."

"It'll be tough, Pete."

"You called me Pete again."

I gave him a withering glare. "Will you stop talking about that cat? That's the third time you've brought him up."

"Yeah, but that's the third time you've called me Pete."

"I did no such thing. Your name is Drover, you may have just lost your tail, and you have more important problems to think about than a sniveling, troublesome cat."

"Okay, I'll try."

"We're lucky to be rid of him, and whatever happened to him, I'm sure he deserved it."

"You're still talking about the cat."

"And besides, you can't expect a cat to live forever. Even if he hadn't been eaten by coyotes, he probably would have died of gluttony."

"What's gluttony?"

"Eating too much. You might recall that every evening at Scrap Time, Pete would go streaking to the yard gate and eat himself into a stupor of gluttony."

"I guess you're right."

"So, as you can see . . ." At that very moment I heard the screen door slam up at the house. My ears shot up. So did Drover's. "What's that?"

"Scrap Time!"

"Holy Smokes, we've got all the scraps to ourselves tonight! Come on, Drover, to the yard gate!"

"What about my tail?"

"Bring it along, we'll look at it later!"

We went streaking past the gas tanks and up the hill, and sure enough we got there first and beat . . . well, actually there was no one to beat, now that . . . we had all the scraps to ourselves, which sort of took a little of the challenge . . .

I slowed down and walked the last ten yards, I sat down in front of the yard gate and Drover joined me.

"Hank, I've got my stub tail back, I'm so happy!"

"Great, glad to hear it. And I'm happy too, for slightly different reasons. With both of us happy, this should be a very happy evening."

Sally May was standing out on the porch, holding a plate of wonderful scraps and gazing off in the distance. All at once she began calling . . . Pete. She called his name over and over.

And on every calling of his name, I . . . well, flinched with happiness, you might say. And wished she would change the subject.

The back door opened again and out came Little Alfred. "Did you find Petey?"

"I'm afraid he's gone," she said, combing the boy's hair with her fingers. "Sometimes cats wander off and don't come back."

"I miss old Pete. I hope he comes back."

"I know, so do I. And maybe he will."

Then both of them began calling Pete's name.

And as if that wasn't bad enough, Little Mister Moan-and-Groan chimed in.

"Gosh, I never thought I'd miss old Pete, but I do."

"Think about all the extra scraps you'll get. Think about your new stub tail. Think about the clouds."

"Okay, I'll try."

After a bit, Sally May stopped calling and gave a big sigh and came over to the yard gate where we were waiting. She scraped the fork over the plate and deposited a delicious-smelling pile of roast beef scraps on the ground in front of us.

"I guess you dogs get it all tonight," she said, then turned and went back into the house. Little Alfred followed her, with his chin down on his chest.

I turned to Drover. "Well, this is True Happiness, son. At last we have all the scraps to ourselves. Now, before you get any big ideas, let me point out that I get the larger portion."

He sniffed the fragrant vapors that were rising from the scraps and ... hmm, very strange ... he shook his head. "You can have 'em all, Hank. I'm not very hungry."

"How could you not be very hungry?"

"I don't know. Somehow food doesn't seem as

interesting when we can't fight over it . . . with Pete."

"Well, you just sit there and watch, and I'll . . ."

Funny, I'd kind of lost my appetite too. I stood over the scraps, sniffed 'em, licked 'em, took a bite and rolled it around in my mouth. The exciting taste I'd expected to find just wasn't there.

"It's not the same, is it, Hank?"

"What?" He'd been watching me. "I don't know what you're talking about."

A tear rolled down his cheek and dripped off the end of his nose. "I wish old Pete would come back and fight with us. Gosh, we might starve to death without him."

I heaved a sigh and pushed myself up to my feet. "All right, Drover, let's go see if we can find the stupid cat."

All at once he was jumping up and down. "Really, Hank, honest? You mean that?"

"I'm doing it as a special favor for you, I want that understood right now. Let's move out. I figger we've got one hour of daylight left."

And with that, we headed north toward the caprock and launched a rescue mission to save . . .

I was still having a little trouble believing this was happening.

CHAPTER TWELVE

Happy Endings Aren't as Simple as You Might Think

We zoomed past the mailbox and headed north. Drover broke the silence. "You don't reckon we might see any coyotes, do you."

"Are you joking?"

He started laughing. "Yeah, I was just joking."

"That was a good joke, Drover, because up in that rough country, the coyotes are as thick as fleas."

All at once it appeared that Drover suffered a blowout on his left front paw. "Boy howdy, this old leg just went out on me, Hank! I was afraid that might happen, I never should have pushed it so hard."

"Hurry up, son, this is a race against time."

He was falling farther behind. "You'd better go on without me, Hank, I don't want to hold you back. I'll see you guys back at the house."

I didn't have time to mess with Drover. The seconds were ticking away, and with every tick of the tock, uh clock, Pete the Barncat was coming closer to . . .

I still couldn't believe I was doing this.

I hit that big sand draw just east of the prairie dog town and followed it north to the base of the caprock. Up ahead, I could see the lone hackberry tree where I'd dumped him off . . . uh, left him . . . delivered him, shall we say.

Since I didn't know what I'd find there, I approached it with maximum caution. Some twenty-five yards out, I slowed to a walk and shifted into Stealthy Crouch Mode. I eased up to a bluff and glanced around in all directions. I peered over the top and saw . . .

Pete the Barncat, surrounded by two hungry-looking coyotes who reminded me very much of two long-limbed, yellow-eyed, slack-jawed, utterly humorless cannibal brothers named Rip and Snort.

Yes, it WAS Rip and Snort, and it had certainly been nice knowing old Pete and I kind of regretted losing him after I had gone to the trouble of running all the way to the caprock, because *nobody takes cats away from Rip and Snort.*

I mean, you talk about guys who love to fight and eat and belch! Those two were champs.

Tough. Double-tough.

So I just lay there on top of the bluff and watched and listened. Hmmm. Pete was sitting and he appeared to be studying the same thing. Staring at the ground.

Snort stood nearby, looking over Rip's shoulder.

That was odd.

All at once Pete extended his right paw and tapped it on the ground, three times, and said, "Mmmm, sorry, Rip, but you sure let that one slip up on you."

Snort began to laugh. "Huh, huh, huh! Brother lose again! Brother got great big dumbness in head. Maybe now we stop and eat," his gaze drifted to Pete, "cat supper!"

"Uh!" said Rip.

"Mmm, let's not rush into anything," said Pete—and you'll notice that he didn't hump up and hiss at those two guys, since that would have made him an instant meatball. "Now let me see. I played Rip and won. I played Snort and won. But Rip and Snort haven't played each other."

"Huh!" said Snort. "Snort not waste time play Chesterless Chester with brother, 'cause brother just big dummy."

Rip scowled and said, "Uh!"

"Oh, I'm not so sure about that," Pete said, flicking the end of his tail, "and if you'll just watch the tail going back and forth, back and forth, to and fro, lull-a-bye and good . . ."

BLAM!

Snort clubbed Kitty over the head with his paw. "Not try funny cat trick on Rip and Snort."

Pete scraped himself off the ground, straightened his ears, and spit dirt out of his mouth. "I'm sure I don't know what you're talking about."

"Talking about cat try to cheat, but Rip and Snort not fall for funny cheating cat trick, huh! Now cat move back and let Rip and Snort play Chesterless Chester, oh boy!" Snort swatted Pete out of the way and sat down at the so-called board. "Brother go first move."

"Uh!" said Rip, and suddenly we had two cannibals staring down at a blank area of dirt and giving total concentration to . . .

Total concentration? Hey, if they were so wrapped up in their . . .

Creeping over the edge of the bluff and extending my body to its fully extended position, I closed my jaws around Pete's head and snatched him into the air. He did a flip and landed on the ground—on MY side of the bluff.

The second he landed, he humped up and bristled and drew back his paw to deliver his usual swat to my nose. Lucky for him, he caught himself just in the nicker of time.

"Mmmm, my goodness, the cops are here!"

"That's right, Kitty. I've come to save your worthless carcass, don't ask me why, but before I do any life saving, I want to hear you say 'calf rope.'"

"Calf rope? Well now, ordinarily cats don't . . ."

"Say it, Pete, or I'll throw you back with the cannibals."

"Mmmm, I'm liking it better all the time. Calf rope, and let's get out of here."

"Hop on my back and hang on!"

He sprang up on my back and we went zooming down the sand draw. We hadn't gone far when I heard a riot starting behind us. No doubt Rip and Snort had looked up from their Checkerless Checker game and had figgered out that they'd been conned by their supper.

And they didn't sound too happy about it. "Uh, stop thief! Not leave with cat! Ranch dog in berry big trouble now!"

Yes, "berry big trouble" indeed, which was a powerful incentitive for me to stretch out my legs and use my incredible speed to move our deal from the caprocks down to headquarters.

I had just begun to pull away from them when Pete turned around in the saddle, so to speak, and faced the back and began talking trash to the brothers.

"Mmmm, you big galoots couldn't catch a flea on a grandpa's knee, and ha ha ha and ho ho ho and hee hee hee, and I'll bet your momma wears old tow sack drawers."

Seemed to me that Pete had a real short memory and real poor judgment, which I guess is standard equipment in your lower grades of cat, and the result was like throwing water on gasoline.

Gasoline on water. Water on a fire. Whatever it is.

Anyways, the brothers got a sudden inspiration to stump a fresh mudhole in the middle of Pete's back, and here they came!

Gasoline on a fire.

"Pete, do me a favor and shut your mouth, will you?"

Fellers, if the chase had gone another hundred yards, we might have been looking at the possibility of throwing baggage overboard to lighten the load, which would have definitely put my new friendship with the cat to a stern test.

But just as the brothers were getting close enough to shorten my tail section, we reached the county road. A truck was coming along and I shot the gap in front of him, made it with inches to spare, and the brothers had to give up the chase.

We had made it!

By that time we were within easy walking distance of ranch headquarters. I slowed to a walk and caught my breath and enjoyed the spectacle of a beautiful Panhandle sunset.

I mean, it was a magic moment. The wind had died to the merest whisper. The western sky had become a fireworks display of red and pink and orange, while off to the north the caprocks were sinking into blue and purple shadows.

I had just pulled off a very impressive rescue mission and had escaped being mauled by the coyotes and had made peace with my very oldest and staunchest enemy.

Just for a moment, it seemed that the whole world stopped what it was doing and joined in on a song to celebrate peace and happiness and friendship and the beautiful sunset. As I recall, it went something like this:

Prairie Vespers

Day is done
Twilight's come
Gone's the sun
And comes the night.
We pray for wisdom
And for health
And for light.

Day is now over
The twilight has fallen
And gone is the sunlight
We're left in the blackness of night
We're praying for courage and wisdom
And for our safe passage from darkness
    to light.

Yes sir, it was an evening to remember. Even Pete caught the feeling of it. "Well, Hankie, you've put me in a very awkward position. Since you saved me from the coyotes, I may be forced to say thank you."

"Yup, you sure might."

"Which cats don't like to say."

"I've noticed."

"And I might even have to start thinking of you as a friend, which really depresses me."

"I know what you're saying, Pete. I mean, just think of all the years we've invested in a lousy relationship."

"Mmmm, I know. All the nasty tricks and hateful names."

"Right, and all the great fights we've had."

"And now it's finished, Hankie, all gone."

"Exactly, wiped out by one thoughtless act of kindness."

"Well, Hankie, we can always hope that it won't last."

With heavy hearts, we strolled into headquarters. As we were passing the yard gate, I noticed that Pete's head shot up and he said, "Mmmm!"

"What?"

"Oh nothing, Hankie. Thanks for everything and now you run along to your gunnysack bed."

"Well, that's sort of what I . . ." I sniffed the air. Mercy, unless I was badly mistaken, the air had just acquired the fragrance of roast beef. "On second thought, Kitty, why don't you run along and find somebody's leg to rub."

"Those scraps are mine, Hankie, because I saw them first."

"Uh no, wrong, incorrect, and wrong. Those are MY scraps."

He humped his back. I growled. He hissed. I barked. He slapped me across the nose and I made a snap at his tail and . . .

All at once I remembered why I'd wanted to bump him off in the first place and things were back to normal and everyone was happy again. I guess.

Fellers, if you can figger out what happiness is in this old life, you're a better dog than I am. I quit.

Have you read all
of Hank's adventures?

1 *The Original Adventures of Hank the Cowdog*

2 *The Further Adventures of Hank the Cowdog*

3 *It's a Dog's Life*

4 *Murder in the Middle Pasture*

5 *Faded Love*

6 *Let Sleeping Dogs Lie*

7 *The Curse of the Incredible Priceless Corncob*

8 *The Case of the One-Eyed Killer Stud Horse*

9 *The Case of the Halloween Ghost*

10 *Every Dog Has His Day*

11 *Lost in the Dark Unchanted Forest*

12 *The Case of the Fiddle-Playing Fox*

13 *The Wounded Buzzard on Christmas Eve*

14 *Hank the Cowdog and Monkey Business*

15 *The Case of the Missing Cat*

16 *Lost in the Blinded Blizzard*

17 *The Case of the Car-Barkaholic Dog*

18 *The Case of the Hooking Bull*

19 *The Case of the Midnight Rustler*

20 *The Phantom in the Mirror*

21 *The Case of the Vampire Cat*

22 *The Case of the Double Bumblebee Sting*

23 *Moonlight Madness*

24 *The Case of the Black-Hooded Hangmans*

25 *The Case of the Swirling Killer Tornado*

26 *The Case of the Kidnapped Collie*

27 *The Case of the Night-Stalking Bone Monster*

28 *The Mopwater Files*

29 *The Case of the Vampire Vacuum Sweeper*

30 *The Case of the Haystack Kitties*

31 *The Case of the Vanishing Fishhook*

32 *The Garbage Monster from Outer Space*

33 *The Case of the Measled Cowboy*

34 *Slim's Good-bye*

35 *The Case of the Saddle House Robbery*

36 *The Case of the Raging Rottweiler*

Join H...
the Cowdog's
Security Force

Are y
you'll
Here

Welc
- A
- F

Eight
- S
- L
- S
- F

More
- S
- A
- U
  w

Total
Howe
shipp

☐ Yes
($8.9
ship.

WHICH
CHOOS

YOUR

MAIL

CITY

TELE

E-MA

Ser

Har
May
P.O.
Per

The
resp
Putn

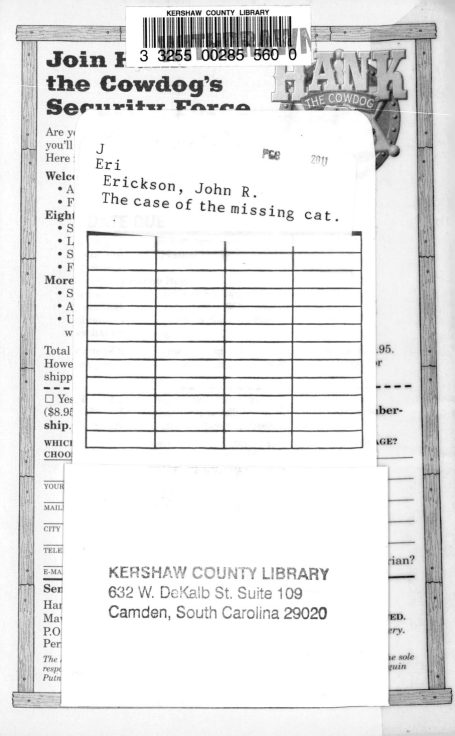